PUFFIN BOOKS

W9-BLU-244

KNOW-IT-ALL GUIDES

HEROIC GREEKS

If being a writer wasn't Nigel Crowle's full-time job, he'd still be doing it for fun. He's written for children's TV series like *Tweenies*, *The Chuckle Brothers* and *Balamory*, and for big stars like Ant and Dec, Elton John, Lenny Henry, Caroline Quentin, Donny Osmond, Basil Brush and Jonathan Ross. He lives in Cardiff with his wife, son and dog where his scripts, plays and books hopefully keep his family:

    (a) occupied
    (b) amused
    (c) in the manner to which they've become accustomed (especially Dexter Dog).

Know-it-All Guides *by Nigel Crowle*

KNOW-IT-ALL GUIDES

HEROIC GREEKS

FAR-OUT FACTS to impress your FRIENDS!

Nigel Crowle

Illustrated by Martin Chatterton

PUFFIN BOOKS

Published by the Penguin Group
Penguin Books Ltd, 80 Strand, London WC2R 0RL, England
Penguin Group (USA) Inc., 375 Hudson Street, New York, New York 10014, USA
Penguin Group (Canada), 90 Eglinton Avenue East, Suite 700, Toronto,
Ontario, Canada M4P 2Y3
(a division of Pearson Penguin Canada Inc.)
Penguin Ireland, 25 St Stephen's Green, Dublin 2, Ireland
(a division of Penguin Books Ltd)
Penguin Group (Australia), 250 Camberwell Road, Camberwell, Victoria 3124,
Australia
(a division of Pearson Australia Group Pty Ltd)
Penguin Books India Pvt Ltd, 11 Community Centre, Panchsheel Park,
New Delhi – 110 017, India
Penguin Group (NZ), cnr Airborne and Rosedale Roads, Albany, Auckland 1310,
New Zealand
(a division of Pearson New Zealand Ltd)
Penguin Books (South Africa) (Pty) Ltd, 24 Sturdee Avenue, Rosebank,
Johannesburg 2196, South Africa

Penguin Books Ltd, Registered Offices: 80 Strand, London WC2R 0RL, England

penguin.com

Published 2006
1

Text copyright © Nigel Crowle, 2006
Illustrations copyright © Martin Chatterton, 2006
All rights reserved

The moral right of the author and illustrator has been asserted

Set in Bookman Old Style
Made and printed in England by Clays Ltd, St Ives plc

Except in the United States of America, this book is sold subject to the condition that
it shall not, by way of trade or otherwise, be lent, re-sold, hired out, or otherwise
circulated without the publisher's prior consent in any form of binding or cover
other than that in which it is published and without a similar condition including
this condition being imposed on the subsequent purchaser

British Library Cataloguing in Publication Data
A CIP catalogue record for this book is available from the British Library

ISBN-13: 978-0-141-32070-0
ISBN-10: 0-141-32070-2

Many thousands of years ago, the Heroic Greeks relied upon their gods for help and guidance to do everyday things. In the same way, and here in the twenty-first century, I rely upon my own family – who are every bit as heroic!

That's why I dedicate this book to them.

Many thanks to my wife, Melanie, the Face That Launched A Thousand Ships, and to my son, Siôn, an athlete of Olympian proportions!

Thanks also to the other members of the Crowle Empire – my ever-supportive mum and dad, Joan and Ken; and also to my niece, Rachel, who loves reading my books to her little brother, Ewan, and to her mum and dad. (That's Helen and my little brother, Neil . . .)

The Ancient Greeks were clever too . . . and so were those friends who lent me books to read about Greek life – particularly Trish Paterson and Andrew Offiler. Susan Gibson and Sue Dye have also encouraged me in my writing over the years, and they've done so in a very civilized manner!

Ancient Greek society was extremely well organized – as, indeed, are my editor, Jane Richardson, and my agent, Sarah Manson.

Finally, it cannot be denied that art was very popular in Ancient Greece – and artists don't come finer than Martin Chatterton, who illustrates all my books so superbly. Thank you, Martin.

Don't forget to flick the top right-hand corner of every page and see me carry the Olympic torch!

*Check out more fab facts at
know-it-all-guides.co.uk*

Contents

So, You Want to Know about . . . Heroic Greeks?

You hold in your hands the ultimate guide to that particularly intelligent and brave race of people – the Heroic Greeks.

Next time you're sweating over a tricky maths question or struggling to remember your lines in the school play, give a thought to the people who made it all possible. After all, if it hadn't been for those darn clever Greeks, we would never have had maths classes or the theatre!

So flick through these pages and learn all sorts of gobsmackingly true stuff you never knew that you never knew about the Greek gods, Olympic athletes and life way back in 1600 BC.

But be warned – every so often you'll find a fact that is complete tosh.

An out-and-out lie. A load of balderdash, in fact! So, that's your challenge – amongst all these amazing facts, can you Find That Fib? You'll be pretty heroic yourself if you do! (And no peeking at the back of the book for the answers!)

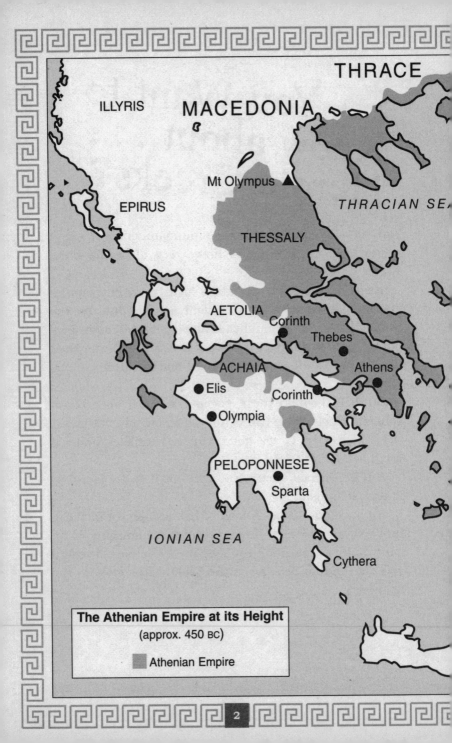

The Athenian Empire at its Height
(approx. 450 BC)

Athenian Empire

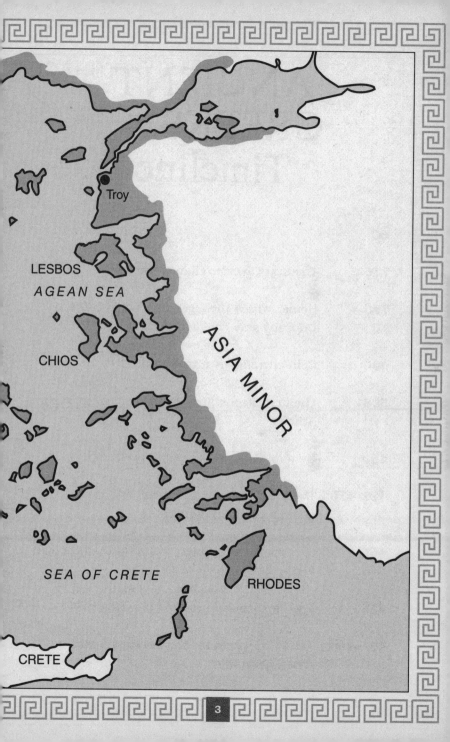

LESBOS

AGEAN SEA

CHIOS

Troy

ASIA MINOR

SEA OF CRETE

RHODES

CRETE

ANCIENT GREEKS – Timeline

BC

776 — The first Olympic Games are held.

750 — Homer writes the legendary poems, *The Odyssey* and *The Iliad*.

600- — Coin currency is introduced.

508 — The first democratic government practises in Athens.

450 — By now, Athens is a very powerful city.

472–410 — Theatre flourishes in Athens and many famous plays are written.

462–429 — Pericles is the popular leader of the Athenian army.

432 — The Parthenon in Athens is being built.

431–404 — The Peloponnesian War between Sparta and Athens begins.

404	Athens surrenders to Sparta.
394	War breaks out between rival Greek states.
338 BC	King Philip of Macedonia becomes the leader of Greece.
336–323	Alexander the Great conquers the majority of the world.
146	The end of the Grecian Empire. Greece is conquered by Rome and is now a part of the Roman Empire.

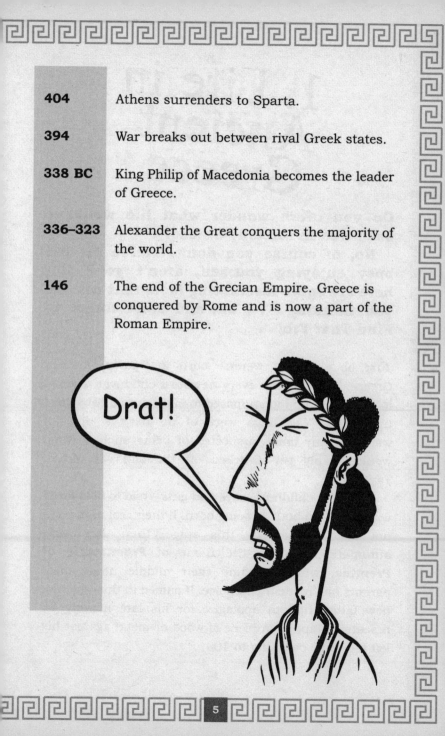

Drat!

1. Life in Ancient Greece

Do you often wonder what life would've been like in Ancient Greece?

No, of course you don't. You're far too busy enjoying yourself, aren't you? But here are some fascinating facts that will get you thinking . . . oh, and don't forget to Find That Fib!

Just be glad you weren't born in **Sparta**, Ancient Greece. That's where every **newborn** child was washed in wine – a tradition supposed to make sure a baby grew up strong. Weaklings were of no use as Spartan warriors. Any child suspected of being such a wimp would simply get chucked off the cliffs at Mount Taygetus.

All Greek children – boys and girls – had to be **named** within half an hour of being born. If their real name had not been chosen by this stage, then they were automatically given the name of **Premistotle** or **Premina**, which became their middle name once parents had made their choice. If named in this way, the new father had to apologize for his late naming by repeatedly tapping a piece of wood or metal against his left toe while counting to 100.

When it came to **baby gear,** the Ancient Greeks were pretty primitive. Imagine a clay chimney pot with two holes on either side. Now imagine a baby stuck on top of it, with chubby little legs sticking through the holes. What is this?

a) a baby's potty

b) a baby harness designed to keep baby out of mischief and in one place

c) a chariot's equivalent of a car seat.

It sounds potty, but the answer is actually a) Greek babies were also fed using a clay baby's bottle, which had a linen or leather teat at one end.

Games Played by Greek Children

Greek children enjoyed many of the games you might today. The top twelve are:

12. Piggyback
11. Leapfrog
10. Ducks and Drakes
    (skimming stones on water)
9. Blind Man's Buff
8. Hide-and-Seek
7. Top-spinning
6. Kites
5. See-saws
4. Dolls' houses
3. Marbles
2. Chequers
1. Knuckle-bones.

A Week in the Life of a Greek Schoolboy

Day 1

Wow! Fantastic! Today is my seventh birthday!

Arggh!! Not so fantastic! Dad's sending me off to school. What sort of present is that? Why can't I be like my stupid older sister? She gets to stay at home to do reading and writing.

Day 2

My family's slave tutor takes me to school. Tchh! Don't my parents trust me? Meet the other eight boys in my class. Some of them giggle when I miss a few notes as I play them the lyre. Teacher is quite stern and reads to us from a rolled-up scroll of papyrus. I practised running in the afternoon, though, carrying a flaming torch. Burnt my fingers a bit.

Day 3

Slave tutor catches me trying to run away from school, as I have decided that I hate arithmetic lessons! Slave tutor drags me back. Boo hiss! Cheer up when I get to do some counting using an abacus – a strange contraption made of pebbles strung across a wire frame.

We practised archery in the afternoon. I need it – I nearly hit my mate Achilles in the heel!

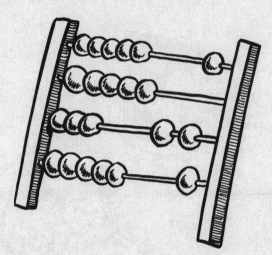

Day 4

Boring day sitting around on stools in front of teacher. We did writing, and we had to use a stylus to write on wooden tablets covered in wax.

In the afternoon, we were encouraged to wrestle one another. It was fun – but we stopped after it got a bit cold, as we had to wrestle without any clothes on!

Day 5

Realize that we only have to do our schoolwork in mornings. Afternoons are when we all go outside to practise our

athletics! I'm better at athletics than I am at schoolwork!
Maybe school won't be so bad after all!

Day 6
Spoke too soon! Teacher has asked us to learn a very long
poem by a chap called Homer. Tried to recite it in front of
Mum and Dad, but I couldn't remember anything other than
the first line! They sent me to bed early!

There's nothing worse than learning verse. . .

Day 7

No school today . . . Hooray! Wanted to do some running games with my mates, but Dad reminded me about poem that I hadn't learnt. Had a bit of a strop and, by accident, stood on my lyre! Dad wasn't happy. I was – now I don't have to do my music practice!

Top Five Pets Kept by Greek Children

5. Dogs
4. Cats
3. Hares
2. Tortoises
1. Goats

Greek girls of twelve or thirteen years old would show they were no longer children by taking their **toys**, like jointed dolls and clay hobby-horses to the **temple**. They'd then offer them to the goddess **Artemis**. Sometimes this was also their **wedding day**.

In actual fact the majority of **brides** were aged fourteen and their husbands were around thirty, having performed national service in the Greek army before settling down to married life.

The Greek philosopher Aristotle actually recommended **thirty-seven** as the best age for men to get married, and **eighteen** years old as the best age for women to marry.

Family Life

Greek men and women not only had separate bedrooms, but quite separate lives. **Women** had **no power** at all, and were expected just to run the household.

Women spent their day at home, spinning, cooking or carrying out other household jobs.

However, a **man** was the **head** of his household and his word was law. A father decided whether to bring up a newborn baby. If the child was ill, or he wanted to save money, he could also decide whether to leave that baby on a hillside to die!

Most households also had **slaves**. Slaves had a pretty bad life in Ancient Greece and had to work very hard.

About one third of the population were slaves, but they had no rights at all, even though they might have been born free and were sold into slavery by mums and dads too poor to care for them. Some Greek slaves had been kidnapped or taken as prisoners of war. They couldn't marry without their owner's permission, and they couldn't own a house. They helped with the day-to-day running of the household, cooking, cleaning and waiting upon their masters.

Another horrible job was to **scrape** the dirt and sweat off wealthy people's bodies after they had coated themselves in oils and herbs. Nice work if you can get it, eh?

I suppose I'm just scraping a living

Rich Greek **businessmen** began their day with a trip to the *agora*, or meeting place in the market, which was the business centre of the city. Equally important, however, was the time a man spent at the *gymnasium*, exercising and bathing and debating anything from art to philosophy. Later, business associates would go off to a dining club, called a *symposium*, taking their own snacks with them in a basket. That's so they could continue talking over their ideas.

What Ancient Greeks Talked About

Which came first – the chicken or the egg?

My fellow Ancient Greeks . . .

Good joke, eh?

I hear you ask me the question . . .

What is the Earth made of?

Greek **houses** were built round courtyards and also had **family shrines** to worship their gods. In fact, at the front of many Greek houses, you'd find a *herm* – a statue of the messenger god, Hermes, who it was believed would act as a guard over the house. The *herm* protected the family from evil spirits.

When the **men** came home after a **hard day chatting** with their mates, they often brought them back for a meal. However, wives and daughters weren't allowed to join them at the table. The menfolk ate and drank the night away in their special area, which was called the *andron*. You'd often find it near the entrance to the house, so that guests who'd drunk one too many litres of wine could stagger off into the moonlight without causing too much disturbance to the household.

Greek **women** had their **own room** too. It was called the *gynaekonitis*, and that was where women entertained their own female friends and looked after the children. It's also where they spun and sewed and made the curtains, cushions, couch covers and clothes for their families.

Ancient Greek Fashion

Women often dyed their **hair** and wore it very long, carefully arranged on top of their heads in an elaborate braidwork of small, tight plaits.

Before marriage, they wore it in long ringlets, but upon gaining a husband they held their hair in place with metal clips or ribbons.

However, they always covered their heads – with their cloak or a veil – when they went outside the house.

Greek men wore their hair fashionably short. They also had beards.

Greeks dressed simply and the **basic Greek outfit** was a rectangle of linen or woollen cloth, which was held in place by a belt and a shoulder pin or brooch. It was called a *chiton* and was coloured red, violet, purple or saffron yellow. They topped it off with a cloak or *himation* – a plain oblong of wool with decorated borders – when they went out.

The women wore an ankle-length *chiton* called a *peplos*.

In the warmer months, children often wore only a length of cloth wrapped round their bodies like shorts.

Greeks walked around barefoot, although occasionally they wore leather sandals or boots.

2. Death in Ancient Greece

Yes, we all know that death is a sad topic. Best not to dwell on it too much. However, if the thought of death depresses you, why not cheer yourself up by Finding The Fib amongst these funereal facts?

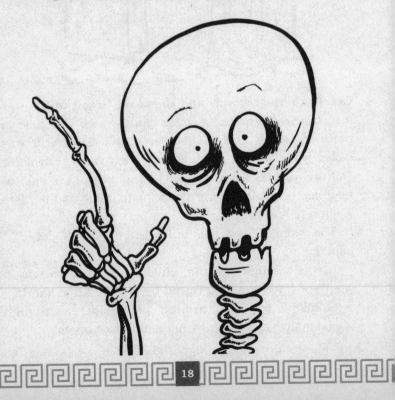

That's gotta hurt!

Aeschylus was a great writer of plays that always ended in death and sadness. However, this tragic playwright met with his own tragic end. It seems that, in 456 BC, an eagle was flying overhead carrying a tasty tortoise for its tea. The eagle was on the lookout for a nice sharp boulder to drop the tortoise on to split its shell open. But it seems the short-sighted eagle mistook the Ancient Greek's bald head for a rock . . . and dropped it on unfortunate Aeschylus instead.

Another strange death was that of top thinker and Greek mathematician **Archimedes** who died on a battlefield, oblivious to a Roman soldier's shouts. The soldier warned him that he was about to get skewered by a sword, but poor old Archie was too busy working out a maths problem in the sand to take notice. (Any maths swots out there – listen and learn!)

Funeral processions in Ancient Greece were led by a hearse. The dead body – complete with wreath on head – had been prepared for burial with sweet-smelling oils from a *lekythoi* or oil flask. The hearse would be followed by a group of wailing women who would beat their chests and tear their hair as they showed their grief.

You could always spot the grave of an **unmarried woman** in Ancient Greece. It was marked by a tall spindly marriage pot called a *loutrophoros*, which was made of clay and decorated with pictures of funerals or weddings. This pot was traditionally given to a young girl to fill her bath with water before her wedding.

Not being married brought great shame upon the woman's family and the vase was used as a symbolic marker.

The Afterlife

Ancient Greeks believed in life after death and the idea of Heaven and Hell.

According to the poet **Hesiod**, how far away was Heaven and Hell?

a) If a blacksmith's anvil fell from Heaven, it'd take nine days for it to fall to Earth . . . and then another nine days for the same anvil to fall from Earth into Hell

b) Heaven was situated above the clouds at Mount Olympus and Hell was under the ground

c) Heaven was in Barbados, and Hell was in New Zealand.

The answer's a). That's pretty far apart!

When someone died, the Greeks believed their souls were ferried by boat across the **River Styx** to the Underworld. The newly deceased paid an *obolus* or Greek coin to **Charon**, the crusty old ferryman who rowed them across. No coin meant no crossing, and Charon would chase them away, condemning those poor souls to restlessly wander the shores of the Styx, and never find peace.

It is still a Greek tradition today to place an *obolus* in the mouth of the recently dead.

Once on the other side, **Hades** – the 'Unseen One' – was a gloomy and terrifying god who either took the soul to a good place or a bad place, depending on how that person had lived life on Earth. Good people went to the **Elysian Fields** and had a happy time, surrounded by their family and friends. Bad people, however, were condemned to a place of constant punishment called **Tartarus** . . . where there really was no rest for the wicked!

Sometimes the head of a Greek household died without having made a will, indicating which possessions he wanted to give to certain family members after his death. If this happened, the property was not given automatically to his family. Instead, all the money went to the keeper of the nearest dog sanctuary, as the Ancient Greeks believed that a dog barking often signalled the precise moment someone died and left this life on Earth. Dogs were therefore treated with great respect.

3. Building the Grecian Empire

The best way to show everyone that you're important is to set up an entire empire! The Ancient Greeks were great empire builders and they constructed all these amazing buildings to prove it. But can you prove which of these facts is a fib?

Coins were popular from the seventh century BC, when they came to Greece after being invented in a place called **Lydia** in **Asia Minor**. Made of gold, silver and a mixture of gold and silver called *electrum*, coins were minted in each city state. For example, coins from **Athens** were minted with the city's symbol of an owl. However, ordinary people couldn't use such expensive coins so they carried on bartering with traders and exchanged goods with each other. They later used **bronze** coins.

Greek Currency
1 Drachma = a standard day's pay – but this was only just enough to live on

100 Drachmae = 1 Mina

60 Minae = 1 Talent of silver

The **Acropolis** was built on a hill overlooking Athens as a home for the warrior goddess **Athena** who gave the city its name. Temples were erected on a site known as the 'Sacred Rock of Athens' during Athens's Golden Age (around the fifth century BC).

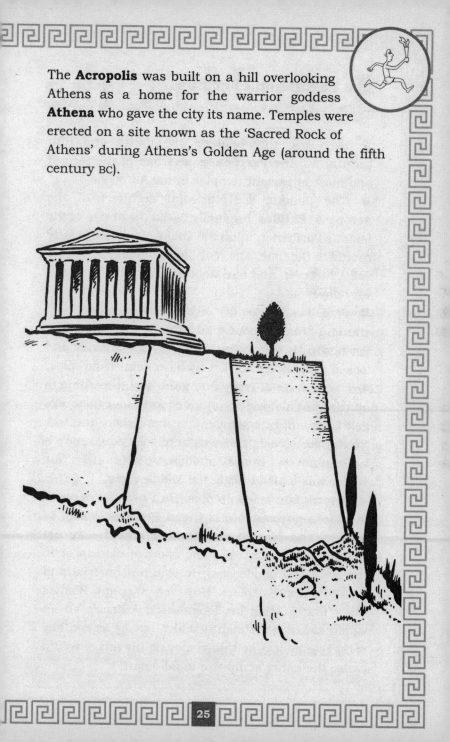

The Parthenon Fact File

472 and 433 BC

● Built probably between the fourth and fifth century BC, the **Parthenon** was one of the largest and most important temples in the Acropolis.

● The famous sculptor and architect of the Acropolis, **Phidias**, originally based the design of the famous Parthenon upon the shape of a popular **jelly mould** of the time. The real-life Parthenon was quite solid, however, and has stood the test of time to this very day.

● Phidias also created a huge twelve-metre high statue of an armour-clad Athena to adorn the Parthenon. It was called the *Athena Parthenos* and looked suitably warrior-like with her helmet and spear.

● It was made of **ivory** and **gold**, and, according to one ancient historian, contained forty-four talents of gold, a quantity equivalent to more than one ton. Converted to cash, this weight of gold would have a value of not less than £7 million. Unfortunately, this statue was looted during the Middle Ages.

● A sorry fate befell Phidias. He'd had the nerve to include a **portrait** of his friend **Pericles**, leader of Athens, and himself on **Athena's shield** – an act which was thought to show massive disrespect to the gods and goddesses. He was put on trial and forced to leave Athens. However, it seems Phidias knew that putting his likeness on Athena's shield would cause resentment – which is why legend has it that he built it so that removing his image would cause the entire sculpture to fall apart!

Statues in Ancient Greece weren't chipped out of marble and then left as bare stone – instead, they were painted in lifelike colours.

Test Your Ancient Greek Column IQ

When we think of Greek buildings, we think of huge columns or pillars supporting their temples. Greeks had three types of column. See if you can match them to their correct image.

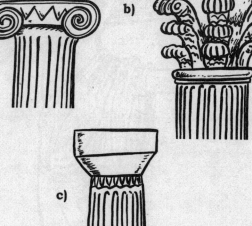

a)

b)

c)

c) *Doric – with a simple capital, as featured in the Parthenon at Athens.*

b) *Corinthian – with a capital or top carved in the shape of acanthus leaves (as in the enormous temple of Zeus Olympius at Athens)*

a) *Ionic – with a scroll-like top called a volute. A good example is in the temple of Apollo at Didyma*

When they weren't building temples to their gods, Greeks were building entertainment venues to watch plays. They built massive **amphitheatres** with stone seating arranged in a semi circle round the stage. An audience of 20,000 watched the entertainment at Athens, and a staggering 30,000 theatre-goers could sit in comfort at Ephesus. Previously, Greek theatre-goers

gathered round the circular patch of ground used for threshing wheat to watch entertainment in praise of their gods, which wasn't quite so posh.

As well as being places of worship, the people of Athens used their **temples** a bit like we use **banks** nowadays. They used to keep the money that they'd collected from around the empire and stash it safely away inside their temple.

4. Inventions and Discoveries

The Greeks were a bunch of right old clever clogs, as this chapter testifies. (Although they did wear sandals, not clogs.) But are you clever enough to Find That Fib?

Seven Things the Greeks Discovered that Helped Mankind

1. Developing basic agricultural crops such as corn, olives, grapes, and ways of processing them
2. Industries using fire, such as pottery and metal-working
3. Carpentry
4. Shipbuilding
5. Writing
6. Systems of weighing and measuring things
7. Methods of counting.

If maths or physics aren't your bag, one thing we can thank the Greeks for inventing is the **world's first shower**. An ancient Athenian vase, from the fourth century BC is decorated with what seems to be the world's first shower, as four muscular ladies wash themselves with water piped from shower-heads shaped like the mouths of lions and wild boars. Many public baths featured showers and fountains, but they were cold. Eeek! Men and women bathed nude in these public baths, which were installed in grand Athenian buildings.

Ancient Greeks also invented **hair curlers**. They curled their hair round clay or terracotta rollers.

Around 330 BC, the Greeks came up with the clever idea of the *clepsydra* or **water clock.** Basically, water was transferred from one cylinder to another, making a pointer move along a scale, showing how much time had passed. Not so much 'tick-tock', as 'drip-drop'! It was, however, very useful as a way of timing Greek citizens when speaking in public and preventing them from droning on and on.

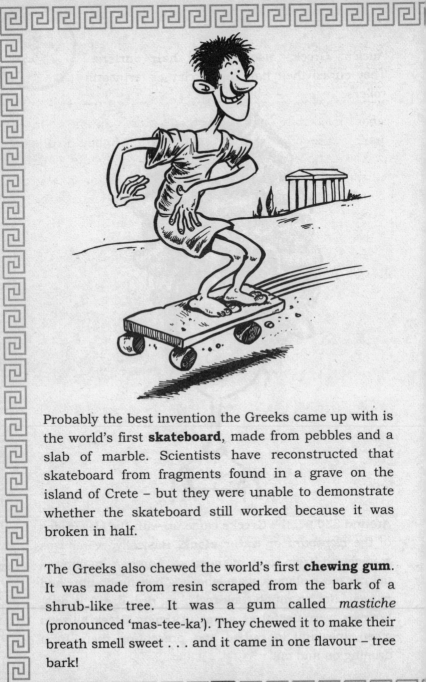

Probably the best invention the Greeks came up with is the world's first **skateboard**, made from pebbles and a slab of marble. Scientists have reconstructed that skateboard from fragments found in a grave on the island of Crete – but they were unable to demonstrate whether the skateboard still worked because it was broken in half.

The Greeks also chewed the world's first **chewing gum**. It was made from resin scraped from the bark of a shrub-like tree. It was a gum called *mastiche* (pronounced 'mas-tee-ka'). They chewed it to make their breath smell sweet . . . and it came in one flavour – tree bark!

Some Ancient Greeks did a lot of thinking and came up with lots of new ideas on astronomy, chemistry, physics and biology. These thinkers were known as **philosophers** and they thought about such things as: if you break a piece of matter in half, and then break it in half again, how many breaks will you have to make before you can break it no further? **Democritus** was known for pondering on this concept and named what all things are made up of – the **atom**.

Some Other Thoughts the Greek Philosophers Had about the World

- **Thales** (*circa* 585 BC) thought the world was made of water.
- **Anaximenes** (*circa* sixth century BC) was Thales's associate and thought the world was made of air.
- **Aristotle** observed that 'flat fish go to sleep in the sand'.

Brainbox **Archimedes** (third century BC) was Ancient Greece's original Nutty Professor and was so caught up in his maths problems that he forgot to bathe. Even when his friends dragged him to the public baths, he drew maths puzzles on his arms in the bath oil. (See page 20 to find out why maths got the better of him in the end.) When Archimedes got into the bath and noticed that the water level rose, he realized why things float. He became so excited that he leapt up and ran naked through the streets of Syracuse, yelling '**Eureka!**' What did he mean by this?

a) **He enjoyed feeling clean again**
b) **He had found the answer to his question**
c) **He had struck gold in his bathtub.**

The answer is b). 'Eureka' means 'I have found it!' Of course, he could have been referring to his rubber duck!

By turning a screw-like machine, Archimedes invented a clever method of defying gravity to **pump water** out of ships through a pipe. Old Archie was also the first person to invent a **crane** with three pulleys.

Four Facts about Plato

Plato was a very clever Greek writer and thinker, and his ideas are still studied by people today.

1. He lived between 427 and 347 BC.
2. His nickname of 'Plato' – meaning 'broad' – came from him having a really broad forehead and an even broader body.
3. His real name was Androcles.
4. He was also a champion wrestler.

Aristotle, an even more frighteningly clever Greek, influenced almost every subject studied in schools today – like mathematics, history, physics, chemistry and literature. If that wasn't enough, he also analysed the anatomies and breeding habits of migrations of 540 animals.

The Greeks' respect for the dead meant that scientists couldn't cut up humans for experiments, but had to use animals instead. Scientist **Herophilus** got around this by conducting some rather **gruesome experiments**. To discover that our arteries actually carried blood round our bodies he cut up criminals – some of whom were still alive at the time!

While the Ancient Egyptians reckoned that we lived our lives through our **hearts**, Ancient Greek medical expert **Hippocrates** disagreed. He worked out that the **brain** was in fact the most important organ in the human body, controlling everything we said or did.

Although **Hippocrates** was the greatest doctor of his day, he and his followers weren't so clever when they thought that illness was due to there being an excess of four liquids – **blood, phlegm, black bile** and **yellow bile** – in our bodies. If those 'humours' were out of balance, a patient got ill. If you were one of Hippocrates's patients, the first thing he'd do would be to take a close look at your 'evacuations' – that is, your **vomit, spit, poo, wee** and **sweat**! Then it was out with hungry leeches or sharp knives to spill some blood – and draw out the illness in the process.

The Greeks studied stars and discovered that the Earth floated freely in space, while turning on its axis. A scientist called **Eratosthenes** not only worked out that the **Earth was round**, but also estimated the **circumference** of the Earth. He did this by measuring the angle of the overhead sun at two places at exactly midday. He did this at Alexandria in northern Egypt and Syene in southern Egypt.

Four Everyday Words in Our Language Coming from Ancient Greek Words

English Word	Ancient Greek Word	Meaning
squirrel	*skiouros*	shadow-tailed
butter	*boutyron*	cow-cheese
pirate	*peirates*	one who attacks
athlete	*athlon, or athlos*	prize or contest

Top Seven Strange Phobias

Phobia is a Greek word meaning 'fear'.

7. *Homichlophobia* – the fear of fog.
6. *Batrachophobia* – the fear of frogs.
5. *Symgenesophobia* – the fear of relatives.
4. *Botanophobia* – the fear of plants and flowers.
3. *Kathisophobia* – the fear of sitting down.
2. *Pogonophobia* – the fear of beards.
1. *Geniophobia* – the fear of chins.

5. Traditions, Festivals and Superstitions

All those centuries ago, festivals and traditions were very important to keep things running smoothly in Ancient Greek society. But be careful – one of these facts is totally untrue. Can you Find That Fib?

Ancient Greek Weddings

As part of the ceremony, the young bride would cut off a lock of her hair which she would then leave on an altar as a gift for the gods.

During the wedding reception, it was customary to cheer on the newly-weds as they leapt around in a large vat of freshly cooked **rice**, performing a traditional **nuptial dance**. The rice was a sign that the couple would be well off in their life together. Once the dance was over, guests were invited to eat a mouthful of the newly trampled rice for luck.

The bride would then be driven from her father's house to her **new home** by her husband. They'd ride in a wagon, accompanied by all their friends and well-wishers, who waved torches and sang. Other friends and family would dance and play instruments like pan pipes, castanets and lyres. Matrons would wail in grief-stricken jealousy, while the menfolk sang in praise of the bride and groom. Even when the newly-weds shut the door of their honeymoon suite, the guests' singing would go on throughout the night.

Worshipping the Gods

The Greek people wanted their **gods** to actually live amongst them, and so elaborate **temples** were built as houses for them. (Turn to page 55 to read more on Greek gods.) Temples were surrounded by four walls, with these all-important elements to keep the gods smiling:

1. A gateway that allowed people to enter the temple.
2. A *cella*, which was a large room inside the temple that held a large statue of the god or goddess, in whose honour the temple was dedicated. That statue faced the entrance doorway so that the god or goddess could 'see' the ceremonies performed at the altar.
3. A sacrificial altar.
4. The outside of the temple building was usually decorated with a number of brightly painted statues.

Temple worshippers had to cleanse themselves with water before praying. Otherwise the gods and goddesses would 'spit back their prayers'!

Poet and historian **Hesiod** recorded this warning about upsetting the gods:

'Not to cut from the five-branched with glittering iron the dry from the quick in the rich feast of the gods.'

What does this mean?

a) Don't ever pinch food from the sacrificial altar.

b) Robes worn in the temples must only be ironed or smoothed out with your fingers.

c) Don't cut your fingernails on a Sunday.

The answer's c)! It seems that even cutting your nails was considered to be doing work on a Sunday, traditionally a day of rest. Also, the person cutting those nails was thought to be a sinner ... and therefore more likely to be attacked by the Devil!

Top Eight Things Offered at a Sacrifice

8. Sheep

7. Oxen

6. Food – everything from grains of rice to complete meals

5. Wine

4. Clothes

3. Locks of hair

2. Pieces of pottery

1. Other personal objects – such as children's toys

Greek Festivals

Festivals were held throughout the year – sometimes to celebrate gods and goddesses, and sometimes to celebrate war victories. Nobody worked during festivals as everyone let their hair down and enjoyed themselves. Most festivals were linked to the farming year, and were held to bless fields and crops.

Every Autumn, the **Festival of Thesmorphia** was held in Athens. It was a three-day women-only festival in honour of the goddess Demeter.

A Girl's Diary during the Festival of Thesmorphia

Day 1

Good to get out of the house for once! I'm getting fed up with all that spinning, cooking and looking after Dad and my brother.

I rounded up my girlfriends and visited the caves around the city, where we'd buried piglets during the spring.

We dug up the pigs' rotten remains, and mixed them with grain. I had to hold my nose the whole time – it reeked! We placed the whole stinking mixture on an altar.

Day 2

The girls and I fasted all day. Spent our time lying or sitting on the ground. (We're not mad – we're just trying to transfer our strength into the soil . . .)

Then we spent an enjoyable evening shouting insults at each other. I know it's tradition, but being hungry makes me quite irritable!

Day 3

Scatter the piggy mixture on the ploughed field. I hope Demeter likes it and our crops grow!

Then it was back to the house, and my dreary routine of spinning, cooking and serving the males in the family.

The **Great Panathenaia** was held every four years in Athens, to celebrate the goddess Athena's birthday. A procession followed a wooden ship that was dragged slowly along on rollers and taken to the Parthenon Temple. In place of the ship's sail fluttered a woman's huge woollen tunic. Upon reaching the temple's enormous statue of Athena, the over-sized tunic would be placed above the statue's shoulders, where it would stay for another four years. After this, at the festival's most solemn moment, cows would be sacrificed and burnt. The meat would be taken back to the city and shared amongst the people of Athens.

Greek youngsters took their first sip of alcohol from the tender age of three.

During the **festival of Anthestria**, priests would let young boys sip wine from clay jugs to show they were no longer infants. Of course, the wine was well watered down so that infant drinkers wouldn't get drunk.

At **Olympia,** there was a special festival for women held in honour of **Hera**, wife of Zeus. Girls competed against one another in running races at this festival, which took place every four years.

The **Ancient Greek calendar** was based around the different phases of the moon. A year was divided into twelve months of twenty-nine or thirty days each, with a new month beginning when the new moon was first sighted at night. The first day of each month was then called New-Moon day, and was the holiest day of each month.

Loony phases of the moon

New Moon

Crescent Moon

Waxing Moon

Half Moon

Full Moon

6. Food and Drink

Here's a lovingly prepared selection of tasty facts . . . but watch out for one that might stick in your throat, because it's a fib! Can you find it?

The Ancient Greeks generally had a **healthy diet**, filled with lots of fresh veggies. Meat was rarely eaten.

A typical Greek **breakfast** consisted of bread and dried figs. A **lunch** might consist also of bread, dried fish, fruit and goat's milk.

Other Things Ancient Greeks Ate and Drank

Quail
Fresh fish
Eels
Lettuce
Beans
Peas
Cabbage
Onions

Leeks
Olives
Meat – such as Deer or Boar – was only eaten at festival times
Cheese
Grapes
Honey cakes

In ancient times, **wine** was drunk well mixed with **water**. It was considered barbaric to drink wine neat – probably because it was so strong. Watering down the wine was often a job for boy servants who'd pour the liquid into a large bowl made of clay, balanced on a stand. Their masters would dip their goblets into this bowl and keep knocking the drink back.

Four Names of Ancient Greek Pots and Vessels

1. *Amphora* – a wine-storing jug, with two handles for easy lifting.

2. *Krater* – a large pot for mixing together the water and the wine.

3. *Kylix* – a wide, two-handled drinking cup.

4. *Oinchoe* – a little wine jug.

After dinner at a Greek house, the merry menfolk played a game called *kottabos*. It was easy to play.

1. Just take your wine *kylix*.
2. Chuck the dregs at a saucer or floating dish.
3. Then settle up the bets on who was closest to the centre.

(A word of warning, however: don't try this at home!)

The Ancient Greeks believed that **olive oil** was a gift from the gods and so, not surprisingly, it was very popular. Not only was it used for cooking, it was also for lighting. What else was it used for?

a) Oiling squeaks
b) For bathing
c) It was often drunk instead of water during droughts.

*The answer is **b)**. Olive oil was also rubbed into the skin as a moisturizer.*

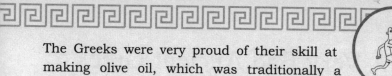

The Greeks were very proud of their skill at making olive oil, which was traditionally a painstakingly slow process. 'Pressers' used to pick up each individual olive between their thumb and forefinger, and squeeze the precious oil out, drop by drop.

The Greeks had their own **fast-food sellers**, who kept them supplied with sausages and pancakes covered in honey.

Those hardened Greeks from **Sparta** made things really tough for their soldiers in training. The poor troops had to eat a repulsive *melas zomos* or **black soup**. This was a broth made from salt, vinegar, and . . . boiled pigs' blood, which gave the soup its attractive black colour!

A Very Bad Ancient Greek Joke about Food

A man from **Sybaris**, which is a city in southern Italy famous for its good living and gorgeous food, saw a Spartan soldier drinking some black soup. Upon being told what went into the concoction, the man from Sybaris said, 'Now I understand why Spartans are brave in battle – they'd rather be killed than drink that black soup!' I told you it was a bad joke!

Greek gods and goddesses typically feasted on **ambrosia**. Though we can't say what it was exactly, we know it was a sweet meal that was supposedly like honey. What's more, it was guaranteed to satisfy the hunger – and the thirst – of any resident of Mount Olympus.

7. The Gods

Like most ancient races, the Greeks told one another stories about their gods. They did this to answer big questions, such as 'Where do we all come from?' The most important question of all, however, has to be 'Can you Find That Fib?'

Mount Olympus was a huge mountain that was the home of the gods. It marked the boundary where the world of mortals ended and the realm of immortal gods started. Its peak was covered in snow and cloud for most of the year, which is why it made a perfect reclusive home for the gods. Mount Olympus is in central Greece, and the mountain's peak is nearly 3 km high.

According to Greek legend, at the beginning of time, the gods who first lived on Mount Olympus were the gigantic **Titans**. The ruler of the Titans was **Cronus**, who was overthrown by the Olympian gods led by **Zeus**. The Titans gave rise to the word 'titanic'.

Handy Guide to the Six Olympian Gods

Assembled on Olympus, there were six Olympian gods.

Zeus – sitting in prime position, was god of weather and king of the gods.

Apollo – god of the sun, truth, healing, music, poetry and dance. He was also the son of Zeus.

Ares – god of war. As the son of Zeus and Hera, he was disliked by them both.

Hephaestus – god of fire, volcanoes, blacksmiths and craftworkers. Son of Zeus and Hera.

Hermes – god of travel, business, weights, measures and sports, and the son of Zeus and Hera. As the messenger of the gods, his job was to guide the souls of the dead to the underworld.

Poseidon – god of the sea, earthquakes and horses. Zeus was his brother.

There were also Six Olympian Goddesses

Aphrodite – goddess of love and beauty. Married to Hephaestus.

Artemis – goddess of the Moon, wild animals and childbirth. She was also the daughter of Zeus.

Athena – goddess of war, wisdom and art. Also called Zeus 'Dad'.

Demeter – goddess of the Earth and soil, grain and fertility. She was Zeus's daughter.

Hera – goddess of marriage, women and childbirth, and all women worshipped her. Also Queen of the gods and goddesses. Not only was she Zeus's wife, she was also his sister!

Hestia – virgin goddess of the hearth, which was the symbol of the house. She was the sister of Zeus.

In time, Zeus's other son, **Dionysus,** the god of wine and theatre, became more and more popular. He eventually took Hestia's place among the Olympians.

Nine Things You Were Supposed To Do if You Were a Greek God

1. You made merry all day, sitting round gold tables.
2. You dined on celestial nectar and ambrosia.
3. You sniffed the fatted cattle being burnt by mortals on their altars below.
4. You listened to Apollo playing his lyre and the singing of the Muses.
5. At sunset, you returned to your home.
6. You had *ichor* – an ethereal fluid – in your veins instead of blood, to stop your body from perishing.
7. If mankind's weapons hurt you, your wounds were healed in record time.
8. You remained young forever.
9. You had the power of metamorphosis – which meant you could turn into animals or objects, whenever you felt like it.

It was considered to be unlucky to make statues of the gods out of wax. This is because sun god, Apollo, used to delight in using his powers to melt any wax statues bearing his image.

Three Nicknames for Zeus – Father of Gods and All Men

Cloud-gatherer
Earth-shaker
Thunderer

As a baby, Zeus had a cradle of gold, played with a golden ball and was brought up in the forests of Ida by which animal?

a) A she-wolf

b) A tiger

c) A nanny goat.

*The answer is c). Zeus was looked after by a nanny goat called **Amaltheia**. She watched over the young Greek god as he fed on meals brought to him by doves and an eagle. Now, is that one spoilt kid, or what?*

According to mythology, Zeus was the **supreme being**, but he could act strangely at times. Just before his first wife, Metis, was about to give birth to their daughter **Athena**, the mighty Zeus swallowed them both – so that they wouldn't be more powerful than him. Shortly afterwards, Zeus had a horrible **headache**. To cure him, his son Hephaestus split open his dad's skull with a bronze axe and out sprang Athena, yelling and shouting and waving a sharp javelin around. Surprisingly, she went on to become Zeus's favourite daughter.

Pan, son of Hermes, was forever acting the goat. He couldn't help himself – largely because he was born with the legs, horns and beard of a goat. When he fell in love with a nymph called **Echo**, and she remained blind to his obvious charms, Pan took drastic revenge and had her torn apart by shepherds. Which is why all that is left is the echo of her voice.

8. Ancient Greek Heroes

Greek heroes included men like Jason, Heracles, Theseus and Odysseus.
They were the nearest that mere mortals could get to the perfection of their gods. Why not do something heroic yourself, and Find The Fib amongst this little lot?

The famous Greek poet **Homer**, who lived around 750–700 BC, wrote two long poem-stories about the heroes of Ancient Greece.

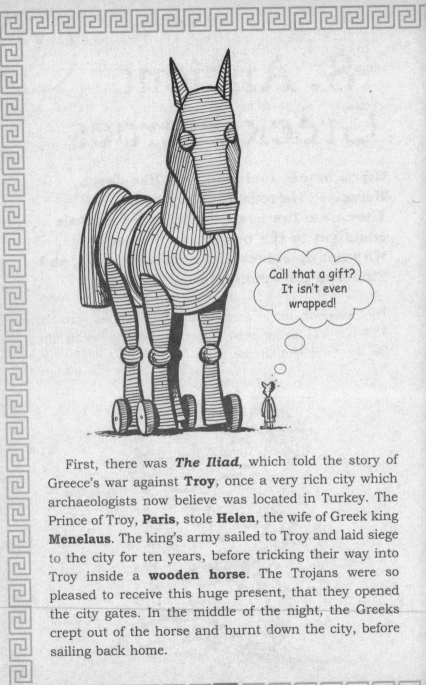

First, there was **The Iliad**, which told the story of Greece's war against **Troy**, once a very rich city which archaeologists now believe was located in Turkey. The Prince of Troy, **Paris**, stole **Helen**, the wife of Greek king **Menelaus**. The king's army sailed to Troy and laid siege to the city for ten years, before tricking their way into Troy inside a **wooden horse**. The Trojans were so pleased to receive this huge present, that they opened the city gates. In the middle of the night, the Greeks crept out of the horse and burnt down the city, before sailing back home.

In Homer's second great poem, **The Odyssey**, he tells of the adventures of a Greek king named **Odysseus**. He had ten years of adventures with monsters, giants and witches. If that wasn't bad enough, he wasn't even recognized when he eventually did return home, and had to chuck out a group of men who'd been pestering his wife, **Penelope**. Nowadays, the word *odyssey* has passed into the English language as meaning a 'long, difficult journey'.

Homer's long poems were all the more remarkable as he was blind.

Heracles was one of Ancient Greece's favourite heroes and many legends sprung up about him (He is also more popularly known as 'Hercules' in Roman mythology). He always carried a huge club around. Being musclebound and athletic, he also inspired the Olympic Games. (For more on the Games, see page 90.) As a sleeping infant, he was attacked by two serpents, but our hero simply grabbed a snake in each hand – and throttled them!

How To Be Like Heracles and Perform His Legendary Twelve Labours

To be a true hero like Heracles, you have to perform the following twelve horrible and extremely difficult tasks – as fiendishly devised by his bitter rival, **Eurystheus**, King of Greece.

1. Skin the Nemean Lion
Shoot arrows at it, then strangle it before skinning. Then wear the skinned skin to make yourself invincible.

2. Slay the Lernaean Hydra
How do you kill a huge snake with nine heads? Start by chopping off one of its heads. Then panic as two more heads grow in its place! Keep your own head, though, and stab the multiplying monster with burning stakes.

3. Trap the Wild Boar of Erymanthus

Some Greeks (King Eurystheus, for one . . .) were so terrified of this monstrous porker that they ran and hid in bronze jars. Here's a tip – Heracles caught it by staying out of the jars.

4. Destroy the Stymphalian Birds

All right, so these monstrous birds have got iron claws, wings and beaks. Simply make a racket by banging cymbals together to scare them. Then fire arrows at them with deadly accuracy.

5. Hunt the Ceryneian Hind

This deer has hooves of bronze and horns of gold. Bring it back alive only by being patient. You'll have to chase it for a whole year.

6. Clean the Stables of Augeias

Here's how to sort out the stinking mess left behind by twelve bulls in a cowshed that's never been cleaned. Simply change the direction of the rivers Alpheus and Peneius so that the water gushes through the building, carrying away all the filth.

7. Capture the Cretan Bull

Visit Crete when it's being terrorized by a mad bull. Capture it and carry it on your back across the sea to Argolis.

8. Catch the Mares of Diomedes

Creep up and kill the guards of Diomedes, who fed human flesh to these horses. Capture the mares. Finally, force Diomedes to eat his own mares.

9. Steal the Girdle of Hippolyte

Visit Hippolyte, the Queen of the Amazons in Cappadocia. Allow those Amazons to steal your weapons. Get annoyed. Slaughter both the Amazons and their queen. Then nick the queen's girdle from round her waist.

10. Ensnare the Cattle of Geryon

Kill the herdsman, the herdsman's dog and the owner of a herd of red oxen. Allow an ox to escape. Wrestle and then kill a king who refuses to return that ox. Herd the cattle together, and sacrifice them.

11. Pick the Golden Apples of the Hesperides

Travel across the world in search of the Garden of the Hesperides. Wrestle, fight and choke a bandit to death. Get attacked by Pygmies. Sew them up in your lion skin. Get chosen as sacrificial victim. Escape. Kill a lot of important people. Shoot an eagle with an arrow. Kill a dragon at the garden gates before picking the apples.

12. Ambush Cerberus, Guardian of the Underworld

To do so, first take an underground journey filled with hazards like earthquakes and falling boulders, and avoid the deathly stare of the Gorgon. Fight loads of Underworld baddies, including Hades himself. Find the dog called Cerberus, the three-headed or possibly fifty-headed monster dribbling black venom and guarding the gates of the Underworld. Half strangle Cerberus with your bare hands.

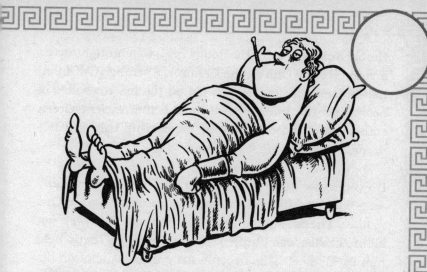

Heracles was unfortunate, however. Having completed the his incredible feat of his twelve Labours successfully, the poor guy **caught a cold** after staying out in the rain for too long. It happened when he was washing himself in a rainstorm, the evening after he'd finished strangling Cerberus the dog. The cold became a **fever** which Heracles battled against for a month before the fever raged more fiercely and he died.

The hero **Theseus** was a great destroyer of monsters like the **Minotaur**, a fierce half-man, half-bull creature. This monster devoured seven girls and seven boys as sacrifices every year. Theseus unravelled a ball of string to find his way through the maze-like **Labyrinth**, killed the Minotaur and retraced his steps using the string. Such a shame, then, that forgetful Theseus didn't change the sails on his boat from black (the sign of death) to white. His father, Aegeus, saw the black-sailed ship returning and thought his son had died in the quest. Distraught, the grief-stricken Aegeus threw himself into the sea . . . oops!

Heroic **Achilles**, he of the dodgy heel, was brought up as a youngster by Chiron the Centaur, a strange half-man, half-horse creature. He was fed on the marrowbones of bears and the intestines of lions – the Ancient Greek equivalent of those disgusting mashed-up baby meals – to make Achilles big and strong.

Do you know how the term 'Achilles heel' came about? As a baby, Achilles was dipped in the River Styx by his mother, **Thetis**, so that he could never die. However, not all of Achilles was dunked into the river, as Thetis held him by his heel. This became the only weak spot on his body. And so Achilles's heel, or weakness, became the obvious target for supreme archer Paris of Troy. Paris shot him in the heel during the siege of Troy, a lucky shot which led to his death.

Things Jason Had to Do to Win the Golden Fleece Owned by King Aeetes

1. Harness a plough with two wild bronze-hooved bulls, who breathed flames.

2. Plough a field and plant it with dragon's teeth.

3. Fall in love with Aeetes's daughter, the magician Medea.

4. Defeat the dragon guarding the Golden Fleece and make off with it.

5. Watch as Medea cuts her own brother's throat, then chops him into pieces.

6. Scatter around bits of Medea's brother to stop her royal dad chasing them.

When **Prometheus** stole fire from the gods, Zeus punished the whole of mankind by sending a fresh calamity to Earth. This came in the perfect form of **Pandora**, whose beauty dazzled Prometheus's brother, **Epimetheus**, who welcomed this gorgeous Greek with open arms. However, guess what Pandora carried in *her* arms? No, not a box, as the saying 'Pandora's box' suggests, but actually a vase. When Pandora raised the lid of the vase, out flew all sorts of terrible evil to infect the Earth. It contained such horrors as disease, greed, old age, death, hatred, violence, cruelty, despair and anger.

The mighty Greek sea god **Poseidon** had a son **Sinis**, who lived at the crossroads of the ancient world, the Isthmus of Corinth on the Northern Greek coast. Sinis had a cruel way of dealing with trespassers where he lived. He used to tie them to the tops of two pine trees he had lashed down. Then he'd cut the ropes and the trees would spring back up – ripping the poor passers-by in two. When **Theseus** heard about this evil practice, the warrior forced sinister Sinis to suffer the same fate.

Top Three Popular Greek Monster Recipes

3. Chimaera – Take the head of a lion, add the body of a goat and mix with the tail of a dragon.

2. Harpy – Take the face of a disgusting old woman, add the ears of a bear and mix with the body of a bird with long, hooked claws.

1. Centaur – Take the body and head of a giant man and mix with the hairy body of an equally huge horse.

The **Cyclopes** were giants with a single eye in the middle of their foreheads. They lived on the south-west coast of Sicily. When the ugliest and largest of the Cyclopes, a giant called **Polyphemus,** fell in love with a beautiful nymph called **Galatea**, he gave her a daily gift of either a bear or an elephant. Awwwww! How romantic!

The sun god **Helios** had a daughter, the goddess **Circe**. She possessed evil magic powers which she used to cast a spell over her island home of **Aeaea**, and turned people who landed on her island into animals. (She even changed Odysseus's companions into swine – Odysseus himself escaped because he chewed a magical herb called *moly*.)

Scylla was a nymph whose beauty made **Circe** jealous. So jealous, in fact, that one day, when Scylla was bathing in a pool, Circe threw magic herbs into the water. Before you could say 'Abracadabra', six huge, long necks sprang from Scylla's shoulders – each with a horrific head on the end. If this makeover wasn't bad enough, each head had a triple row of teeth, enabling this grotesque Greek to snack on unwary sailors.

9. Making Decisions

Ancient Greeks were very keen to make their people decide upon important issues of the day. Like them, you have to make a decision – can you Find The Fib?

Ancient Greece was a country made up of a number of separate city states – each one called a *polis*, and based round a city. Each *polis* included all the surrounding houses, villages and farms. Each of these cities had groups of people who had different roles to play in society at that time.

Polis is where our word 'politics' comes from.

> **The Polis in Ancient Greece**
> **– The Four Most Powerful**
> Athens
> Sparta
> Corinth
> Thebes

Most of our knowledge of Ancient Greece comes from Athens – the centre of all the most beautiful buildings and sculptures. Athens gave us the idea of **democracy** – government in which all citizens have a say. However, other city states were becoming just as powerful – such as war-loving Sparta, to the south. Across the Aegean Sea there were many rich Greek colonies – all of which were keen to learn more about science, art, architecture, medicine, writing and literature. Greek civilization flourished but as the cities competed with one another for land, trade and glory, the rivals began fighting amongst themselves. This bitter warfare ended only when the Macedonian king, *Alexander the Great*, defeated Greece.

Greek Citizens

The Ancient Greeks believed very strongly that their people (well, the menfolk, anyway . . .) could take their share in the decisions, the rights and the duties of the city.

Handy facts about Greek citizens

- Citizens had most rights – they were the property owners, and took part in issues of law and property.
- Most citizens were males – and were more respected in Grecian society than women, children or foreigners.
- In Sparta, you had to be rich to be a citizen – which meant only one in ten men could afford the privilege.

The Greek Assembly

Greek men were encouraged to stand up and have their say. Every Greek citizen could vote in their Assembly, or place where the laws were made, on important issues such as going to war and how their city should be governed. This made the city a democracy, where a number of people had a say. By the fifth century BC, this meant that 43,000 people could vote in Athens alone.

If you paid a small fee, you could speak and cast your vote. However, if you didn't turn up, slaves holding ropes dipped in **red paint** would round you up. The Assembly fined anyone with red paint on their clothes.

To throw someone out of the Assembly, you simply scratched their name on a piece of broken pot or a discarded scallop shell. If the same name appeared on too many pieces – that person was simply banished. Oh well – that's politics for you!

There were no judges or lawyers to conduct trials in Ancient Greece. Instead, **juries** of up to 500 people were selected by drawing lots and made their judgement in a trial. The jury decided whether someone was innocent or guilty by dropping small **discs** into a pot. Hollow discs meant that you were found not guilty. Solid discs meant that you'd been found guilty, and were put before the court for sentencing.

If convicted, a criminal was rarely jailed. They were either forced out of Greece, lost voting rights or had property taken from them.

But to find out the answers to *really* complicated questions, Greeks visited an **oracle.** An oracle was a prophet or person who would divine the future. One of the most famous oracles was at **Delphi**, where **Pythia**, a priestess, would go into a trance and mumble a reply which could only be worked out by another group of priests. In ancient times, Pythia was so famous that people travelled far and wide to visit her.

The shrine of Delphi became so popular with visitors that the queue was often days long. One enterprising farmer, **Thargelion of Mekademon**, used his oxen to cut a steep groove down the sloping hillside nearby. He then diverted a stream to run down this groove and charged waiting crowds a small fee to amuse themselves by sliding down his water slide.

Every Greek army had its **soothsayer** (known in Greek as a *mantis*), whose predictions were carefully listened to, even whilst the battle was raging.

For example, at the **Battle of Plataea**, the Spartan army waited patiently even though the Persians were throwing a stream of missiles at them. They were determined to wait until the *mantis* had carried out the correct rituals!

The oracles were taken very seriously, but everyone knew that you had to think hard about what was **really** being said in these predictions.

For example, the Lydian king **Croesus** was supposed to have sent to the oracle at Delphi, asking whether or not he should go to war against the Persians.

The oracle told him in reply that if he crossed the **River Halys**, he would **destroy a powerful kingdom**. Croesus thought this meant that he would destroy the Persian kingdom and he carried on with his invasion.

It was only after he and his army had been defeated by the Persians, that he realized that when the oracle had talked of the defeat of a powerful kingdom in the prediction, it had meant Croesus's own kingdom was under threat of being crushed!

10. Arts and Entertainment

Those multi-talented Greeks were always putting on plays or making music, or telling stories. What a bunch of show-offs, eh? Let's see if you can show off your fib-finding skills by deciding which of the following stories is complete tosh.

Storytellers in Ancient Greece were called *rhapsodoi* – a word which actually meant 'song-stitcher'. That's because these talented men literally stitched together a poem-story in a new way as they told it, without changing its meaning.

It's where our English word 'rhapsody' comes from, which means a state of rapture or an epic poem or musical composition. And while we're on the subject, a poet was a maker – with the Greek word *poeio* meaning 'to make', and our word 'rhythm' comes from their word *rhythmos* which means 'an easy flowing of harmony or sound'.

The Ancient Greeks loved going to the **theatre**, especially in Athens. They'd spend the whole day in the theatre watching three plays in a row. As the seats were made from stone, they'd take their own cushions to sit on, and also a packed lunch!

Some Facts about Ancient Greek Theatre

● All the actors in Greek plays were male, and played even the female roles.

● The word 'theatre' comes from the Greek word *theatron,* which meant 'a viewing place'.

● **Thespis** was the first playwright to write dialogue for actors, around 534 BC – which is why we call actors *thespians,* in his honour.

One theatre – at **Epidaurus** – survives to this day, and modern plays are still performed here. It was built with an auditorium which can seat 14,000 people on stone seats.

Some Greek playwrights – like **Aeschylus**, **Euripedes** and **Sophocles** – wrote **tragedies**, or serious plays based around the myths of Greece.

Other Greek playwrights – like **Aristophanes** – wrote comedies, plays poking fun at gods and politicians of the day.

During the fifth century BC, it was popular for acting troupes to be made up of Greek **prisoners**. These criminals had won the right to leave jail so long as they performed in plays to entertain the masses. As a consequence they often wore sack-cloth bags over their heads while onstage so that they couldn't be recognized and chased by crowds when they weren't performing.

The Greeks also loved to **sing**. They sang at ceremonial occasions such as weddings, births and funerals, of course, and also to help them through boring jobs like grinding grain. And they had songs to cure people who were ill. One young singer, keen to protect his voice before an important choral event, admitted to having **washed his throat** down with the **sticky slime** that covers a conger eel – Yuck!

Dionysus was a god with double responsibilities, being the god of **wine** and **drama**. He was once turned into a goat for his own protection, and so a poem was written in his honour and sung by a chorus of goats.

The Ancient Greek Public's Favourite Entertainers

Musicians	Magicians	Jugglers
Acrobats	Sword-swallowers	Fire-eaters
Actors	Poets	

According to Homer, the herdsmen's god, Hermes, invented the musical instrument we know as the **lyre**. It was made from the shell of a dead tortoise which had been scraped out. This shell then had holes drilled in it, and arms of animal horns or ivory, with animal hide stretched over its open side.

Finally, this frame was strung with seven strings of twisted sheep's gut which was plucked away to make music.

Typical Greek Musical Instruments apart from the Lyre

Aulos – a pair of pipes, made of hardwood or bone
Syrinx – pan pipes, or reeds cut of varying lengths, bound with wax and string
Kithara – a more booming, deeper version of the lyre with a wooden soundbox
Trumpets, tambourines and cymbals – which were also used in battle

As a musical bunch, it's only fitting that 'music' is a word invented by the Greeks. It comes from the word *mousike* which covered not only playing instruments and singing, but also arts and literature, dancing, poetry and sculpture.

Other Words Greeks Invented

How many do you know?

Melody	Tone
Harmony	Baritone
Symphony	Tonic
Polyphony	Diatonic
Orchestra	Diapason
Organ	Chromatic
Chorus	Syncopation
Chord	

From at least 4 BC, the Greeks had a system of notes for writing **musical scores** on papyrus. The Greeks sometimes played musical instruments on their own, but mostly they were used to accompany the human voice.

11. The Original Olympic Games and Sports

How could we celebrate the achievements of the Greeks without mentioning the Olympics? Simple, we couldn't, so here they are – apart from one, which is a downright fib!

The Greek Olympic Games were held at the Olympia site in **Elis**, western Greece. It was a great **athletic festival** held in honour of Zeus and Hera. Since around the fifth or sixth century BC, the early Olympic Games were held in mid-August, about the time of the first full moon after the Summer Solstice – possibly the hottest time of the year in Greece! Scientists in Texas reckon that temperatures around 12 August soared as high as 39°C.

That's probably why, according to Greek legend, the first marathon runner **dropped dead** as soon as he completed his run – he was suffering from heatstroke.

His name was **Pheidippides**, and in 490 BC, he sprinted the 26 miles (46 km) from Marathon to Athens to announce a Greek victory in battle against Persia, before keeling over dead.

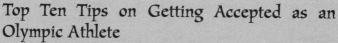

Top Ten Tips on Getting Accepted as an Olympic Athlete

1. Don't be late – the only excuse for missing training is being shipwrecked!
2. Train at the city of Elis for a full month, before competition begins at the nearby valley of Olympia.
3. Appear in front of a twelve-strong, purple-cloaked judging panel.
4. Take an oath before a statue of Zeus – swear you've trained for the past ten months, and you'll do nothing to bring the Games into disrepute.
5. Compete fairly – don't try and bribe the judges.
6. Be relatively fit and able to take part in the competition.
7. Eat sacrificed wild boar.
8. Take off your clothes (you will be competing in the nude).
9. Draw lots to see who you're competing against.
10. Avoid dysentery or dehydration and get ready for three days of intense sport.

Timetable for Early Olympic Games

Day 1
- Chariot racing
- Other horse-related events (for example – bareback riding, riding without stirrups, cart-races with mules)

Day 2
- Pentathlon consisting of:
- Running
- Jumping (for example, Long Jump)
- Throwing the discus
- Throwing the javelin
- Wrestling

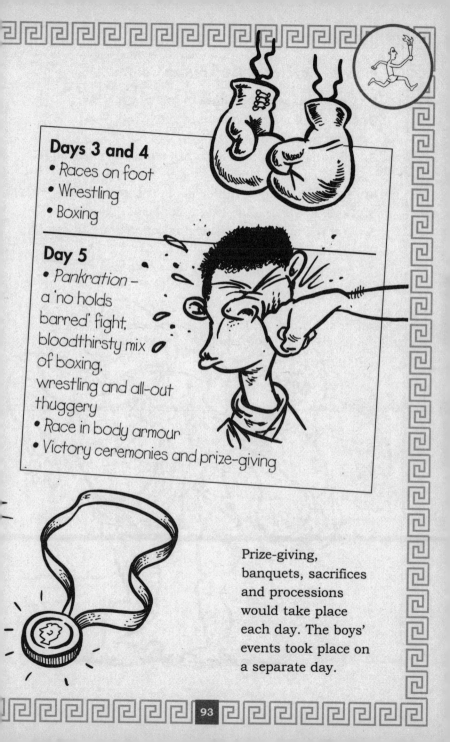

Days 3 and 4
• Races on foot
• Wrestling
• Boxing

Day 5
• Pankration – a 'no holds barred' fight, bloodthirsty mix of boxing, wrestling and all-out thuggery
• Race in body armour
• Victory ceremonies and prize-giving

Prize-giving, banquets, sacrifices and processions would take place each day. The boys' events took place on a separate day.

How to Referee a *Pankration* Contest

1. Do not allow competitors to bite one another.
2. Do not allow competitors to gouge out each other's eyes, nose or mouth.
3. Allow competitors to kick, hit, strangle or beat up their opponent.
4. Beat competitors with sticks to separate them.
5. Don't use a clock to time a contest.
6. End the fight when the losing competitor sticks a hand up to surrender. Or dies!
7. Award wreath of laurel leaves to the victor.

Young girls could be spectators at Olympia. However, married women weren't allowed to watch the Olympics and some historians reckon that this is because male athletes competed in the **nude**, which they believed made them **run faster**. It may have started in 720 BC when athlete **Orsippos** sprinted to victory, despite having lost his loincloth en route!

To help them jump further, athletes in the **Long Jump** used to hold lead or stone weights when they swung forward during take-off, and then backwards upon landing.

Some of the **long-distance** champions were considered to be so much faster than their fellow runners that they were given long brass **trumpets** to blow as they raced. If they didn't sound a continuous **note** as they crossed the finishing line, they were immediately disqualified. In other words, they'd blown it for not having blown it!

Virgin females were allowed to compete in the games. One of the first female Olympic champions was **Princess Kyniska** from Sparta who was the owner-trainer of a twice-winning chariot racing team in the early fourth century BC.

Boxers in Olympic events didn't wear gloves – only leather **thongs** tightly wrapped round their hands. Some boxers supposedly added **metal studs** to these fist-bindings – making them a bit like knuckledusters. Ouch!

In 404 BC, proud mum **Kallipateira dressed as a man** to watch her son take part in the Olympic boys' boxing event. She was so thrilled when her son won that she jumped a fence and revealed her female identity in the process. Because she was the daughter and sister of past Olympic champions, she was pardoned from being punished by death.

The Winners

What would Olympic winners be presented with?

a) A tub of olive oil/margarine substitute

b) A martini with an olive garnish

c) A laurel wreath

The answer is c). But in athletic games held in Athens, champions were given pots of olive oil.

Not only would the winners get a prize, but an **Olympic victory parade** would be staged, and the winning athletes wore a woollen headband as they headed towards the Temple of Zeus. Along the way, they were pelted with a ticker-tape parade of flowers, twigs and fruit by an appreciative crowd. There would also be a celebratory feast.

Top Four Perks of Being an Olympic Winner

Winning Olympic athletes really were the celebrities of their day. They also enjoyed:

4. Being allowed to wear purple robes.

3. Free meals in the town hall.

2. No paying of taxes.

1. A statue in their image made and put up in Olympia.

The worst case of **bribery and corruption** within the games took place in AD 67, when the nutty Roman Emperor **Nero** decided he wanted to enter the Olympic chariot race. But there was a problem – the Olympics weren't scheduled to take place that year! Nevertheless, nervous officials decided to hold them – just to keep Nero happy. He fell from his chariot, however, and didn't finish the race. Nevertheless, corrupt officials (bribed with money and Roman citizenship) judged Nero to have won the race. Lucky Nero won 1,808 first prizes at that year's Olympics – and he didn't even compete in several events!

Other Sports in Greece

Other than the Olympics, there were many other games and sports played in Greece. As you find out about them, don't forget to Find That Fib!

Top Four Non-Olympic Games

Other than the Olympic Games at Olympia, there were also other popular games:

The Isthmian Games at Corinth

The Pythian Games at Delphi

The Nemean Games near Argos (that's Argos near Nemea in Greece, not in your high street).

The Greeks played an ancient version of **hockey**, using curved sticks to hit a ball made from a **pig's bladder**.

They also played a strange sort of catching game where two pairs of men faced one another, each pair being made up of a man sitting on another man's shoulders.

Athletes would begin at **starting-lines** and dig their feet into special grooves to get a racing start. Sometimes a stadium had a starting gate that would spring open to commence a race – much like we have in a horse race. However, if an Ancient Greek runner made a false start in a running event, he was in danger of being flogged. That's because his irritated trainer also carried a whip and would lash out if their young charges had ruined their chances of winning a race by taking off too early.

Homer wrote an early **sports report** in his famous ballad poem, the *Iliad*. He described how Odysseus came from behind and won a race because the leading runner **Aias** slipped on some cow dung – an offering from the cow sacrificed at the start of the Games!

Homer also made the world's first literary reference to a **chariot race** as he described the **funeral games** of Patroclus. Diomedes, Eumelus, Antilochus, Menelaus and Meriones took part in this race, which was one lap round the stump of a tree. It was won by Diomedes, who received a prize of a slave woman and a cauldron.

Boys and girls on the island of **Crete** had an unusual, if dangerous, way of keeping fit. They'd wait till a **bull** charged them, and at the last moment they'd leap up and grab the bull's horns. Then, in a stunning athletic display, they'd somersault over its back.

Greek chariot races became a popular and spectacular sport. In some races, over **forty horses** competed at the same time on four-horse chariots, racing twelve laps of a course measuring around 400 metres. As a result, **deadly collisions** were quite common. In two-horse chariot races, drivers only had to race eight laps round the course – however, the bends were sharper and more dangerous as a result.

Prizes – for male and female champions – included large jars, or *amphorae*, of expensive **olive oil**, and specially dedicated pieces of **pottery**. In fact, 140 amphorae of olive oil were given to the winner of a four-horse chariot race at the first Panathenaic Games in 566 BC. In other games, city states gave their own prizes to athletes – like exemption from tax or free living quarters.

12. Wars and Battles

It seems the Greeks were forever waging wars. Are you ready to battle it out and discover which of these facts is actually the fib?

The Ancient Greeks were a proud nation, and they actually seemed to enjoy going to war. . . especially with one another. Although only Sparta had a permanent army, the other city states would call up their citizens to go into battle. Usual military tactics were to walk towards the enemy, then charge them at the last minute. Sheer weight of numbers would hopefully make the enemy scatter. Those hardy Spartans, however, would walk up to their enemies at a steady pace – and with flutes playing. Then they'd refuse to retreat!

The Greek **battle season** lasted from March to October. This meant that, after surviving months of fighting, the war-weary soldiers would return home in time to do some back-breaking work such as harvesting olive and grape crops.

Greek soldiers were known as hoplites or 'armed men', from the word *hopla* which meant 'shield'. Generals trained their hoplites to march **shoulder to shoulder**, sword in right hand and shield on left arm. In this way, each hoplite was protected by the shield of the soldier marching next to him and no arrows or spears could penetrate the phalanx of advancing soldiers. During battles, hoplites had to keep bravely marching forward in step. If any soldier panicked and lost his nerve – or sense of rhythm – the whole line broke up and left them vulnerable, allowing the enemy to attack.

Only Greeks who were rich enough to buy their own bronze armour became hoplites. They were also known as *Zeugitès*, which meant 'owners of oxen'.

The **trireme** was a Greek sailed warship, rowed by 170 oarsmen in three rows – one above the other. It was very fast and far superior to the **penteconter** with only one row of 50 oarsmen, and to the **bireme** with its double bank of oars.

The trireme was particularly good for **ramming**, a rather nasty Greek war tactic. The oarsmen were ordered to row at full speed, and aim themselves squarely at the enemy ships!

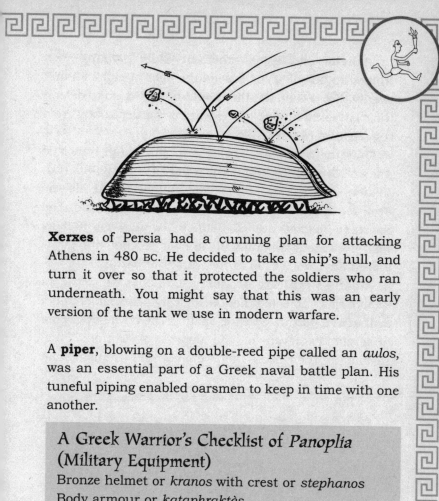

Xerxes of Persia had a cunning plan for attacking Athens in 480 BC. He decided to take a ship's hull, and turn it over so that it protected the soldiers who ran underneath. You might say that this was an early version of the tank we use in modern warfare.

A **piper**, blowing on a double-reed pipe called an *aulos*, was an essential part of a Greek naval battle plan. His tuneful piping enabled oarsmen to keep in time with one another.

A Greek Warrior's Checklist of *Panoplia* (Military Equipment)

Bronze helmet or *kranos* with crest or *stephanos*

Body armour or *kataphraktès*

Bronze shin pads or *proknèmis*

Arm protectors or *cheir*

Cloak or *chlamys*

Tunic or *chiton*

Short iron sword or *akinakès*

Spear with iron tip or *hyssos*

Bronze shield, or *chalkaspis*, with armband or *porpax*

Leather sandals or *krepis*

In **Athens** and some other city-states, young men trained to be soldiers between the ages of eighteen and twenty. From then on, they could be called up to defend their city-state in one of the wars or battles that were a regular part of Greek life.

Only the **Spartans** – being a rough, tough bunch of Ancient Greeks – had their own full-time army. Spartan soldiers were so well-trained that there was scarcely any need for officers telling them what to do in battle. The Spartans reacted out of instinct – which was just as well, because it was difficult to hear officers' orders (or indeed anything at all) in the uproar of battle.

Sparta's **military academy** took boys as young as **twelve** and subjected them to a lifestyle almost as tough as that of a mature Spartan soldier. The boys never wore underclothes, even in the depths of winter. When sleeping in their beds, they were covered by rushes not nice warm duvets. And they washed themselves in icy cold rivers all the time. They learnt to blindly obey orders – and if they didn't, they were flogged!

Spartan Soldiers' Pre-battle Ritual

1. They would strip naked and exercise.

2. Then they would oil down their bodies and comb out each other's long hair.

3. They also took small sticks, and wrote their names on them before tying them to their arms. This was an ancient form of soldiers' **dog tags** that would allow their bodies to be identified if they were hurt or perished in battle.

The **bow and arrow** were vital Greek weapons. Bows were made of wood, sinew and animal horn, and could fire arrows up to 180 metres.

Spartan mothers were supposed to be as hard as the fathers. It may be just a popular story told about these **tough mums**, but it seems one of them was so keen to instil obedience, bravery and duty in her offspring that she waved her son off to battle, telling him to come back from the war 'either with your shield, or on it!'. She'd only accept him as a warrior, proudly returning with the shield on his arm, or being carried back from war, lying dead on it!

13. Find
That Fib . . .
Answers

Chapter 1. Life in Ancient Greece

Did you believe that nonsense about naming a newly born child within half an hour of birth, otherwise it was called Premistotle or Premina? Or about proud dads whacking wood against their toes as a result? No – of course you didn't, cos that was a Big, Fat Fib.

However, the truth is that a Greek child did remain nameless until ten days after its birth. A naming ceremony in the presence of relatives of both parents was then held, complete with drinking and dancing.

Chapter 2. Death in Ancient Greece

I hope you weren't taken in by that rubbish about dead people giving money to Ancient Greek dog homes – or dogs barking at times of death. That was the fib, and I hope you spotted it! However, it is true that on the death of the head of a Greek household, all the family property was shared between his sons. If he didn't have any children, he could adopt a relative so that the riches didn't get taken away from the family.

Chapter 3. Building the Grecian Empire

Congratulations if you spotted that the Parthenon wasn't built on the shape of a traditional Greek jelly mould. That was the Fib, and you Found It!

The Parthenon, was, however, built wholly of expensive marble – like the Erechtheum at Athens – and this was a luxury few cities could afford. The word 'Parthenon' comes from the Greek word *parthenos*, which means virgin or maiden.

Chapter 4. Inventions and Discoveries

Bad luck if you believed that nonsense about Ancient Greeks inventing the first skateboard. It was an out-and-out lie! However, around 100 BC, an Ancient Greek engineer called Heron (or Hero) came up with an idea for the first steam engine. Actually, it wasn't so much an engine, more a rotating ball powered by steam . . . which is probably why the Greeks called it *aeolipile* which means 'wind ball'.

Chapter 5. Traditions, Festivals and Superstitions

By the way, did you believe the stuff and nonsense about cheering on newly married Greek couples as they danced around in a large vat of freshly cooked rice? I'm afraid that was the Fib you were looking for! However, at Greek weddings, it was actually customary to throw nuts, fruits and sweetmeats – not rice like today – at the happy couple, as these were symbols that they would be well off in their life together.

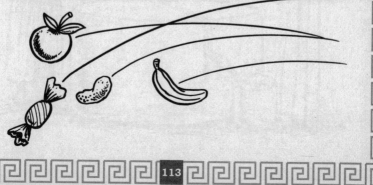

Chapter 6. Food and Drink

If you didn't believe the fact about the olive-oil pressers squeezing olives by hand, then congratulations! You Found that Fib!

However, it *is* true that Greek farmers used a pressing machine to extract oil from the olives they grew. Olives were crushed with stone rollers to release their precious oil, and the mixture was ladled into sacks which were then pressed again to ensure that as much olive oil was extracted as possible.

Chapter 7. The Gods

I do hope you realized that the sun god Apollo wouldn't go around melting statues of himself that had been made out of wax! That was the Fib . . . and I hope you found it! However, Apollo, being a sun god, did – according to Greek legend – make the fruits of the earth ripen, and protect crops by destroying mice and locusts.

Chapter 8. Ancient Greek Heroes

Don't believe the story of Heracles dying of a cold which became a fever? If you guessed that, then you Found That Fib! However, legend has it that the Greek hero actually died when he wore a poisonous tunic, made by the centaur Nessus.

Chapter 9. Making Decisions

If you believed that silly story about a water slide being made at the shrine of Delphi, then shame on you! It was a Fib!

However, it is true that the shrine of Delphi was close to a grove at the end of an ancient cobblestone trail called the *Kalki Skala*, or 'evil stairway'. This led to two peaks from which anyone who'd said anything disrespectful about the gods was thrown to his death.

Chapter 10. Arts and Entertainment

So . . . did you really think that Greek actors were criminals who wore sack cloth bags over their heads on stage? You did??? Whoops! That was the Fib!

However, Greek actors did indeed wear masks on stage because lighting in theatres was so poor that the audience weren't able to see the actors' actual faces. Some were made of stiff linen with real hair for beards, and some were made of clay. The masks also contained a device which helped actors to project their voices.

Chapter 11. The Original Olympic Games and Sports

Finding the Fib among that little lot must've been something to blow your own trumpet about! Yes, the piece about Olympic runners having to blow a brass trumpet as they crossed the finishing line was completely made up.

However, it's a fact that pipe music was actually played during the Olympic events, to help athletes relax and achieve their best at competition.

Chapter 12. Wars and Battles

Did you see through that piece of nonsense about Xerxes of Persia attacking Athens by making the first tank out of an upturned boat? That was the final Fib in the book! However, it is true that a 'wall of wood' was used to defend Athens in 480 BC, in a battle against the Persians and as predicted by the oracle at Delphi. At least 100 triremes, or fighting ships, lined up to protect supply lines.

Join

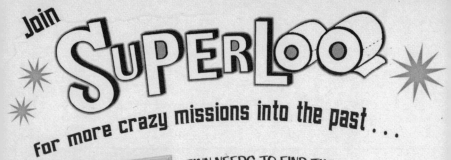

SuperLoo

for more crazy missions into the past...

FINN NEEDS TO FIND THE LEGENDARY GOLDEN TOILET OF KING TUTANKHAMUN – CAN HE PASS HIMSELF OFF AS AN ANCIENT EGYPTIAN TO GET IT BACK?

SUPERLOO HAS TAKEN FINN TO ROMAN BRITAIN WHERE CONSPIRACIES ARE AFOOT INVOLVING GLADIATORS, BEARS, VERY FIERCE BRITISH TRIBES AND, OF COURSE ...HADRIAN'S FAMOUS LATRINE.

Can Superloo escape capture and termination?

What will its next mission be?

Will Finn change his mind and go with it?

FIND OUT IN SUPERLOO'S NEXT TOILET QUESTS:
HENRY VIII'S PRIVY & **QUEEN VICTORIA'S POTTY**
COMING 2007

puffin.co.uk